Maisie Dappletrot Saves the Day

Daisy Meadows

ORCHARD

Magic
Animal Friends

Special thanks to Valerie Wilding

ORCHARD BOOKS

First published in Great Britain in 2016 by The Watts Publishing Group

1 3 5 7 9 10 8 6 4 2

Text © Working Partners Ltd 2016
Illustrations © Orchard Books 2016

The moral rights of the author and illustrator have been asserted.
All characters and events in this publication, other than those clearly in the public domain,
are fictitious and any resemblance to real persons, living or dead, is purely coincidental.

A CIP catalogue record for this book is available from the British Library.

ISBN 978 1 40834 106 3

Printed in Great Britain

MIX
Paper from
responsible sources
FSC® C104740
www.fsc.org

The paper and board used in this book are made from wood from responsible sources

Orchard Books
An imprint of Hachette Children's Group
Part of The Watts Publishing Group Limited
Carmelite House, 50 Victoria Embankment, London EC4Y 0DZ

An Hachette UK Company
www.hachette.co.uk
www.hachettechildrens.co.uk

Map of Friendship Forest

Joollyhop Shop

Harmony Hall Theatre

Petal Hill

Garland Green

Cherry Tree Corner

Treasure Tree

Bluebell Brook

Agatha Glitterwing's Shop

Slipperslide's Home

Sparklepaw Cottage

Coral Cove

Summer Sands Beach

Grizelda's Tower

Witchy Waste

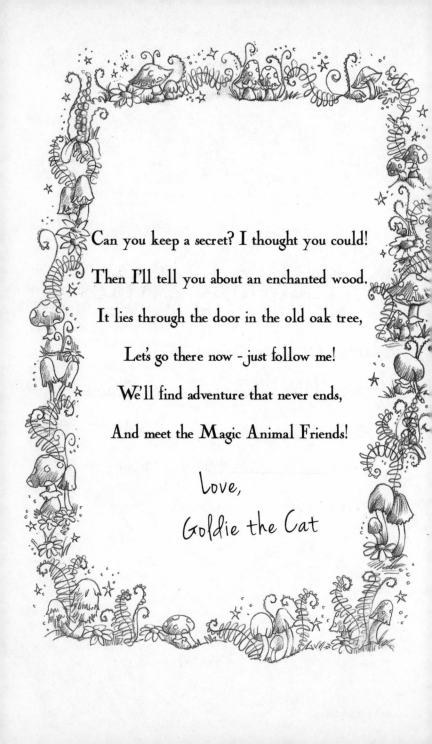

Can you keep a secret? I thought you could!

Then I'll tell you about an enchanted wood.

It lies through the door in the old oak tree,

Let's go there now - just follow me!

We'll find adventure that never ends,

And meet the Magic Animal Friends!

Love,
Goldie the Cat

Story One
Lightning Strikes

CHAPTER ONE

The Start of Spring

At Helping Paw Wildlife Hospital, Lily Hart and her best friend, Jess Forester, were planting carrot seedlings in a vegetable patch.

Lily looked over the fence at two ponies. They stood beneath a shady tree, swishing their long grey tails.

 9

"I wish the carrots could grow extra quickly so we could give them to the horses," Lily said.

"Me, too," said Jess, pressing soil around one of the seedlings. "I bet some crunchy carrots would help them feel better."

The young horses were two of the patients at the wildlife hospital, which was run by Lily's parents in a barn in

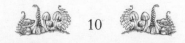

their garden. Jess lived across the road, and she came over whenever she could to help care for the animals. All around them were pens filled with other animals who were getting better. In one pen, three baby rabbits dashed around in the spring sunshine, their fluffy white tails bobbing. In a run beside them, two guinea pigs squeaked as they nibbled the grass.

"We should plant lettuce and cucumbers, too," said Jess. "Then the animals would be able to eat all their favourite things, just like they do at the Toadstool Café!"

The girls shared a smile. The Toadstool Café was in a magical place called Friendship Forest, where the animals lived in little cottages and ran little shops – and they could all talk! The girls' special friend, Goldie the cat, lived in the forest and took the girls there for all kinds of amazing adventures!

Lily drew in a sharp breath. "Look!" she cried, pointing to the horses' field.

A beautiful golden cat bounded across the grass and jumped onto the fence.

"It's Goldie!" Jess cried. "She must have come to take us to Friendship Forest!"

The girls hugged her and stroked her soft fur. With a mew, Goldie leaped down and bounded towards Brightley Stream, at the bottom of the garden. She jumped across the stepping stones and ran into the meadow.

Jess and Lily raced after her. In the meadow they came to an old, lifeless tree – the Friendship Tree!

Lily and Jess glanced at each other excitedly. They knew what would happen next, and they couldn't wait!

The Friendship Tree's branches were bare, but as soon as Goldie reached it the

 13

leaves sprang to life, and
buds popped up on every
twig. Yellow primroses and
purple violets bloomed in the
grass below, while butterflies,
bees and baby birds fluttered
busily all around.

It was so beautiful,
and suddenly the air
was filled with the
sweet smell of a
sunny spring day!

When Goldie put a paw to the trunk, letters appeared in the bark that spelled out two words.

"Friendship Forest!" the girls read.

Instantly, a door with a leaf-shaped handle appeared in the trunk.

Following Goldie into the shimmering glow, the girls felt their skin tingle all over, as if they were inside a glass of fizzing lemonade. They knew they were shrinking, just a little.

As the light faded, the girls found themselves in a sun-dappled glade in Friendship Forest. Usually there were flowers everywhere, and petals of every colour nodding in the gentle breeze. But today there were no flowers, just leaves on the trees and bushes.

"Welcome back!" said a soft voice.

Jess and Lily turned to see Goldie. She was now standing upright, almost as tall as they were, with her glittery scarf around her shoulders. The girls hugged her tightly.

"It's lovely to be here again," Jess said.

"But the forest looks strange without any flowers," Lily added.

Goldie smiled and pointed to a bush.

When the girls looked more closely, they saw that it was covered in plump buds that looked ready to burst open. Buds hung from the branches of the other trees and bushes, too.

"Don't worry, there will be lots of flowers soon," said Goldie. "That's why I got you. It's a special time in Friendship Forest – Beautiful Bloom Day!"

"What does it mean?" Lily asked.

"For the buds to open, one of the Friendship Forest families has to perform some very special magic today," Goldie explained. "Would you like to see?"

The girls grinned.

"Definitely!" said Jess.

Goldie led them through the forest, and finally they reached a pretty cottage in a sunny clearing. The cottage had lacy curtains billowing at the windows and the top half of the door was open.

"It looks a bit like a stable," said Lily.

The girls followed Goldie to the side of the cottage, where three carts were lined up. There was a big blue one, a big yellow one and a small red one.

"It *is* a stable, isn't it?" cried Jess. "Does a horse family live here?"

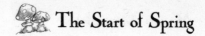

As soon as she'd spoken, they heard the clackety sound of hooves. From the back of the cottage trotted a pretty grey and white Shetland pony, pulling a cart.

The girls grinned in delight as they recognised her from their adventure with Mia Floppyear the bunny.

"Hello, Mrs Dappletrot!" cried Lily.

"Why, hello, girls!" Mrs Dappletrot called. "Welcome to our home!"

Jess tugged Lily's sleeve and pointed at Mrs Dappletrot's cart. Lily gasped out loud as she saw it – it was a pile of sparkling jewels that glittered in the sun!

CHAPTER TWO

Watch Out for the Unicorns!

Mrs Dappletrot trotted over to give the girls a nuzzle hello. "It's so lovely to see you both again!" she said.

"What beautiful jewels!" Jess said. "Are they magical?"

Mrs Dappletrot said, "I'll tell you all

21

about them. But first come and meet my family."

She called through one of the stable windows. "Auntie Dappletrot! Lily and Jess are here!"

Another pony trotted out. Her coat was glossy brown, like a conker.

"Nice to meet you," she said. "I've heard all about you two!"

Mrs Dappletrot slipped out from the harness that attached her to the cart and trotted to the edge of a field that was next to the stable. "Maisie!" she called.

Jess and Lily turned to see a pretty foal

playfully chasing after
a butterfly. When she
heard her name, she
galloped over and
skidded to a
stop. Her
coat was
a lovely
toffee

colour with creamy white patches, and
she had a stripe down her nose the colour
of vanilla ice cream. She was wearing
a bright garland of flowers around her
neck. Even for a Shetland pony, she was

very small – she was only a little higher than the girls' waists.

"Hello, Maisie," said Jess. "I'm Jess and this is Lily."

"Hello!" said Maisie.

Just then, the butterfly perched between Maisie's ears and fluttered her blue wings. "You'll never catch me!" the butterfly said in a tinkling voice. "I'm too fast!"

"I will next time, Flora!" Maisie giggled. "I'm practising running," she explained. "One day I'll be able to

24

run as fast as Auntie and Mum."

"You certainly will," laughed Mrs Dappletrot. "Now, today is Beautiful Bloom Day – so we Dappletrots have work to do."

She trotted back over to the heap of dazzling gemstones. There were round ruby red ones, long emerald green ones and yellow ones that shone like sunshine.

"They're so beautiful!" Lily sighed.

"Are they yours?" Jess asked.

"They belong to Friendship Forest," said Mrs Dappletrot. "They're called Grow Gems. On Beautiful Bloom Day, we fill our carts with Grow Gems and go around the forest, putting one at the foot of every tree, bush and plant. The Grow Gems' magic makes all the buds open."

"Wow!" said Lily.

"Look at Mum and Auntie's necklaces," said Maisie.

The girls looked. The two ponies both wore magnificent green jewels hanging around their necks on silvery chains.

"Only ponies wearing green jewels know where Grow Gems are found," Maisie explained. She looked at her hooves. "I really hope I get mine soon."

Mrs Dappletrot smiled. "One day, Maisie. But you're

helping this year, aren't you?"

Maisie nodded uncertainly. "I'm so small, though. I hope I don't slow you down." Then she lifted her nose. "I won't slow you down!"

"Of course you won't," said her mum. "Let's ask Goldie and the girls if they'll help us, too!"

"Would you?" Maisie asked eagerly.

Jess and Lily glanced at each other. "We'd love to!"

Mrs Dappletrot tapped her hooves in a special rhythm, and suddenly all of the glittering gems flew into the two big carts.

"Wow!" Jess gasped.

"The Dappletrots have special magic – that's why they're the only ones who can scatter the Grow Gems." Goldie explained.

Instead of Grow Gems, Maisie fetched lots of pretty flowers and piled them into her cart.

"Well remembered, Maisie," her mum said. "We always get very hungry while we sprinkle the gems!"

"These are Filling Flowers," Maisie told the girls. "They'll keep us full up for ages."

When the carts were full, the ponies trotted into the harnesses, ready to start pulling.

Maisie stamped her hooves in excitement. "Let's go!"

Mrs Dappletrot went first with the girls in her cart, then Auntie, who pulled Goldie in hers.

Lily glanced back to see Maisie was a little way behind, her tail swishing as she trotted, pulling her tiny cart behind her.

"I'll catch you up!" Maisie called. "Keep going!"

After a while, Mrs Dappletrot stopped by some bushes that were covered with green buds the size of plums.

"Let's start here," she said. "We can wait for Maisie to catch us up."

Auntie Dappletrot stamped her hooves in a special rhythm, and a cluster of Grow Gems floated from the cart and sprinkled the ground under the bushes. Immediately, the buds opened into beautiful starflowers.

"Wow!" said Jess.

"Amazing!" said Lily, with a gasp.

 31

Goldie and the girls climbed out of the carts to admire the flowers. Suddenly, the peaceful stillness of the forest was broken by the sound of thundering hooves.

Lily frowned, confused. "Is that Maisie? It sounds too loud."

Mrs Dappletrot looked worried. "No pony sounds like that," she said.

A black chariot burst through the trees. It was pulled by three unicorns who snorted crossly, stamping and tossing their heads. The Dappletrots, Goldie and the girls had to leap back out of their way.

Standing in the chariot was a tall,

bony woman wearing a purple tunic over skinny black trousers. "Stand still, unicorns!" she shouted, yanking the reins.

"Oh, no!" cried Lily. "Grizelda!"

Grizelda was a horrible witch who was determined to drive the animals away from Friendship Forest, so she could have

it for herself. So far, Goldie and the girls had managed to stop her nasty spells, but they were sure she'd never give up.

"You girls again?" Grizelda sneered. "Meet my new helpers. This is Lightning!"

A white unicorn with a black horn tossed his head. He disappeared in a flash of white light, then immediately reappeared again.

The girls blinked in amazement.

"Here's Thunder!" Grizelda snapped.

A black unicorn with a white horn stamped his foot, making the ground rumble and shake. Jess and Lily clutched each other, and the two ponies whinnied in fright.

"And this is Stormcloud!" said Grizelda.

A grey unicorn with a grey horn whisked his tail and rain began falling from the sky, making the ground muddy under their feet.

Grizelda cackled. "With my unicorns, there'll be no blooms in Friendship Forest today!"

Jess and Lily stared at her bravely. "You might have unicorns, but we have ponies!" Lily said, looking at the Dappletrots.

"Not for long!" Grizelda snarled.

 35

She pointed a skinny finger at the ponies.

Jess and Lily's eyes were dazzled by a brilliant flash. They blinked, then stared around the clearing in horror. There were two carts filled with Grow Gems – but Mrs Dappletrot and Auntie Dappletrot had vanished!

CHAPTER THREE

Speedy Weed

"Bring our friends back!" cried Jess.

Grizelda shook her head, making
her green hair twist around like snakes.
"They're somewhere they'll never be
found," she cackled. "Now for the next
part of my plan. Unicorns!" she shrieked.
"Destroy those gems!"

 37

Grizelda let go of the unicorns' reins and they charged at the two carts. To the girls' horror, they kicked the carts with their hooves, turning them over. The Grow Gems tumbled out.

The unicorns stamped on the glittering gems, smashing them into tiny pieces.

"Stop!" Lily cried, but the girls and

Goldie had to leap clear of the thrashing hooves and flying shards.

When the unicorns stopped, there was only shimmering powder left.

Grizelda cackled with delight. "No more Grow Gems means no more flowers, and no food on the Treasure Tree for the animals to eat! And now for the third part of my brilliant plan – I think it's the best bit!"

She held up a sack and took out a round, prickly object, the size of a grape.

"Do you silly creatures know what this is?" she demanded. "It's a Speedy

Weed seed! Soon there'll be Speedy Weeds
everywhere and the forest will be so
horrible that all the animals will have to
leave!" She took the unicorns' reins once
more. "And I'll have Friendship Forest to
myself at last!"

"Never!" cried Jess.

But Grizelda just shook the reins
and the unicorns sped away, taking the
chariot with them.

For a moment, Lily and Jess stood
staring after her. Goldie's green eyes were
wide with shock. Then there was a rustle
from the trees behind them.

The girls turned to see Maisie trot into the clearing, pulling her little cart. She looked at their shocked faces and her eyes swam with tears.

"What's happened?" she wailed. "Where's Mum?"

Lily and Jess rushed to cuddle her as they explained what Grizelda had done.

"If I was faster then I could have stopped her," Maisie sobbed.

"If you'd been here then Grizelda
would have cast her spell on you as well,"
said Lily, stroking Maisie's mane.

"That's right," said Jess. "So it's good
you weren't!"

"Don't worry," said Goldie. "We'll find
your family. Won't we, girls?"

The girls nodded. "Of course!"

Maisie blinked her tears away and
shook her brown mane. "And I'm
going to help you," she said. She gave
a determined stamp of her hooves. "I'm
going to get my family back!"

"Look!" Goldie pointed to a bush.

One of Grizelda's Speedy

Weed seeds was underneath it,

shaking from side to side. "What's

happening?" she cried.

The seed suddenly sprouted. Spiky

shoots grew out of it and twisted over

the bush.

Jess held her nose. "It smells

disgusting. Like smelly socks …"

"And rotting cheese …" said Lily.

"And stinky pondweed," said Goldie. "And look how quickly it's growing!"

Within moments, rust-coloured Speedy Weed had smothered the bush. Beneath nearby trees, more seeds shook as their spiky shoots appeared.

"Oh, no!" cried a faint voice.

"Listen!" said Maisie. "I think someone's in trouble!"

"It sounds like it's coming from the Treasure Tree!" Goldie said in alarm. "Let's go!"

The girls tore after her, with Maisie and her little cart close behind. The Treasure

Tree grew all sorts of fruits and nuts, and the animals got most of their food there. It was the tallest tree in the forest, so they saw the top of its branches before they reached it. They were completely covered in Speedy Weeds!

Lily gasped, horrified. "Where will the animals get their food now?"

As they ran through the forest, they could see Poppy Muddlepup, Chloe Slipperslide and some other animals all gathered around the Treasure Tree.

"Oh, no!" cried Poppy. "That weed's covered the creamy peaches!"

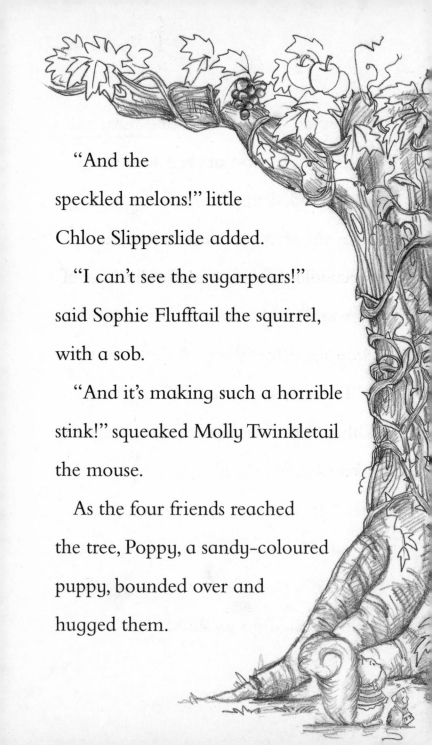

"And the speckled melons!" little Chloe Slipperslide added.

"I can't see the sugarpears!" said Sophie Flufftail the squirrel, with a sob.

"And it's making such a horrible stink!" squeaked Molly Twinkletail the mouse.

As the four friends reached the tree, Poppy, a sandy-coloured puppy, bounded over and hugged them.

Chloe the otter ran over, too, her shell necklace jangling as she went. She reached up to cuddle the girls and Goldie. Lots of worried animals gathered around the magical tree.

"I'm so glad you're here!" cried Chloe. "Do you think you can save the Treasure Tree?

"We'll do our best," said Lily.

"Come on," said Jess. "Let's tear down this Speedy Weed."

She grabbed a thick, rust-coloured stem and pulled, but it was too strong.

"Let me try!" said Maisie.

She stomped and stamped on the nearest weed stem, breaking it in half.

"Hooray!" the girls cheered.

But the broken pieces of Speedy Weed wriggled and joined back together.

All around them, the weeds were smothering the forest.

Lily turned to Maisie. "We will rescue your family, we promise," she said. "But first, we've got to save the forest – before it's too late."

 48

CHAPTER FOUR

Quite Contrary Potion

Poppy Muddlepup was carefully sniffing the Speedy Weed seed at the base of the Treasure Tree. Then she stared at it thoughtfully.

Jess nudged Lily. "Of course! Poppy's family grow magical plants in their garden! Maybe she'll know what to do."

 49

When Poppy turned around, she was
wagging her tail with excitement.

"I've seen seeds like this before," Poppy
said. "Mum and Dad get rid of
them with a Quite
Contrary potion!"
Jess hugged
her. "Brilliant!
How do we
make some?"

"It's really easy," Poppy said. "We'll
need to mix up some water with a plant
that's the opposite of the Speedy Weed,
then sprinkle it over the seeds."

"So, because Speedy Weeds grow so quickly, we need something that grows slowly?" asked Goldie.

"Exactly." Poppy beamed.

Maisie danced from hoof to hoof. "The Filling Flowers I brought for a snack take ages to grow!" she exclaimed. "Do you think that will work?"

Lily smiled. "They sound perfect for the Quite Contrary potion," she said.

But Maisie's head drooped.

"What's wrong?" Jess asked.

"I lost the flowers when I ran to catch up," she said. "They fell out of my cart."

 51

"Don't worry," Jess reassured her. "We can get some more."

"But how?" Goldie wondered. "There are Speedy Weeds all over the forest."

Maisie cantered around in an excited circle. "I know where Mum picks them," she said. "Hopefully the Speedy Weeds haven't grown there yet. This way!"

"I'll get a tub to mix the potion in!" Poppy said as the girls hurried after Goldie and Maisie.

"We'll find you back here soon," Lily called over her shoulder.

They ran through the forest, dodging

around the prickly, smelly weeds. They
had grown so quickly that the treetops
were thick with them. They even shut
out the sunlight, so everywhere was dim
and gloomy.

The little pony led them between two
holly trees, around a blackberry bush,
down a slope, then stopped. Ahead of

them was a patch of shimmering flowers.
Each was pale pink with long, delicate
petals. The smell was delicious.

"Those are the Filling Flowers,"
Maisie told them.

But Lily and Jess stared at the
flowers in dismay. They were
surrounded by thick walls of
prickly, smelly Speedy Weed!

"Oh, no," cried Jess. "How
are we ever going to make the
potion now?"

Maisie stamped her hooves.
"I have to try!" she said. "I might

54

not be very fast at running – but I am good at jumping!"

She unhitched her cart, backed up a little and charged.

"Come on, Maisie!" yelled Jess. "You can do it!"

Maisie galloped down the slope. Then she jumped, stretching out her legs as she sailed through the air towards the wall of Speedy Weeds.

Lily and Jess both held their breath.

"Go, Maisie!" Goldie shouted.

Maisie gave a neigh as she soared upwards – right over the wall of weeds!

She landed in the middle of the beautiful
Filling Flowers.

Goldie and the girls cheered. "Hooray!"

Maisie picked lots of the shimmering
flowers with her mouth,
then turned around to
jump back. She looked
worriedly at the weeds
all around her – without
much room, Maisie
couldn't get as good a
run-up as before.

"Oh, dear," muttered
Jess. "I hope she makes it!"

Maisie leaned backwards then charged, flinging herself up into the air. She went over the Speedy Weeds, jumping over so narrowly that her tail almost caught on the prickles. But she landed safely beside Goldie and the girls.

"Yay!" Jess yelled, throwing her arms around Maisie's neck.

"You did it!" cried Lily.

Maisie dropped the buds into her cart. "More!" she panted. "Must get more!"

With the others cheering her on, Maisie jumped back and forth. She didn't stop until her cart was full of beautiful buds.

"That was amazing!" said Lily.

Maisie grinned. "I just don't like giving up," she said.

Goldie placed the final bunch of flowers in the cart. "Now to save Friendship Forest!"

CHAPTER FIVE

Fixing the Forest

Poppy Muddlepup and Sophie Flufftail were waiting near the Treasure Tree with a big tub of water for mixing the potion.

Everyone grabbed Filling Flowers from Maisie's cart and tossed them into the tub.

"The petals need to be mixed into the water," said Poppy.

 59

Jess glanced around at the gloomy, weed-covered forest. "We'd better hurry," she said. "Nearly every leaf is covered by the Speedy Weeds now."

"We need to spread the potion around the whole forest," Goldie said.

Just then, a voice called, "Hello, below!"

It was Captain Ace the stork, with a rope in his beak. He was towing his patchwork hot-air balloon.

The balloon
came down
close to the
weed-covered Treasure Tree.

"Young Poppy told me about Grizelda's spell," said Captain Ace, "and I've seen what it's done to our forest. Why don't you fly over it in my balloon and sprinkle your potion from above?"

Goldie, Maisie and the girls were all thrilled.

"Come on, let's mix the potion as fast as we can," Jess cried.

"I can do it!" said Maisie.

She jumped into the tub, stamping and stomping until the water and flowers squished into a thick, pink liquid.

"Good job, Maisie," said Lily.

They were about to lift the tub into the balloon's basket when the sky flashed.

"Oh, no," said Jess. "It's a storm!"

"Worse!" said Lily. "It's one of the horrible unicorns!"

A moment later, Lightning crashed through the trees! The white unicorn snorted angrily, tossing his head. "So you think you can stop Grizelda's plan?" he whinnied. "Well, I've come to stop YOU!"

He pointed his horn at Captain Ace's balloon. There was another flash of light and

the

balloon

was gone!

Lightning

reared up on his

hind legs.

"Try to fly that balloon now! Your little forest is doomed!"

With a final toss of his head, he cantered off.

The girls ran to comfort Captain Ace the stork, who looked very bewildered. The rope he had been holding had completely disappeared.

"I can feel the rope," he squawked, "but I can't see it, or my balloon! He must have turned it invisible."

"That horrible unicorn's right," said Sophie, with a sad sigh. "We can't save the forest now."

Maisie stamped her hooves. "Yes, we can!" she cried. "I'll carry the potion on my cart! I know I'm not very fast, but I'm sure I can do it."

"Of course you can!" said Jess.

"And we'll all help," said Lily. She and Jess carefully picked up the tub full of potion and put it onto Maisie's cart. "We can all sprinkle it around the forest. Working together will make it quicker!"

"And I know where we should start," Jess said. She tipped the potion over the Speedy Weed seed at the bottom of the Treasure Tree.

65

The seed shrivelled and shrank. Then, with a puff of rusty-brown smoke, it vanished. The weeds that had been growing out of it fell away from the Treasure Tree, revealing the fruit and nuts, and huge buds, that hung from all of the branches. Then the weeds vanished, too,

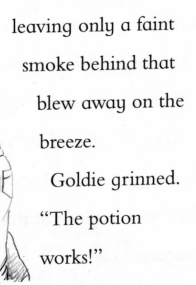

leaving only a faint smoke behind that blew away on the breeze.

Goldie grinned. "The potion works!"

Everyone cheered.

They set off, running alongside Maisie. The girls and their friends filled their hands with potion from the tub, then dashed among the trees, sprinkling the potion over the Speedy Weed seeds.

There were happy cries all over the forest as the nasty seeds vanished in puffs of smoke and the weeds shrivelled away.

"The forest's green again!" said Lily.

After what seemed like hours of work, they were all panting for breath. Maisie's sides were heaving and she was hot from running so hard.

"Do you want a rest?"
Goldie asked her.

Maisie shook her head. "I'm
not stopping until we've finished!"
she said. "And I think there's only
one tree left to save now."

Lily and Jess followed Maisie's
gaze. All the trees around them were
free of Speedy Weeds – except for the
tall tree in the centre of the forest.

It had lots of seeds at the bottom,
and was so covered in
Speedy Weeds that

it took a moment for Lily
and Jess to recognise it.

"Oh, no! It's the Friendship Tree!"
cried Lily. "We have to fix it – or we
won't be able to go home!"

Jess and Lily looked at each other,
feeling frightened.

"Don't worry!" Maisie said.
She unhitched her cart
and kicked backwards,
overturning the tub so the
potion drenched

the seeds at the foot of the Friendship
Tree. In a puff of smoke, the Speedy
Weeds disappeared.

Lily hugged the little foal. "Well done,
Maisie!"

"We've saved the forest!" cried Goldie.

"And it's all thanks to you," added
Jess, hugging Maisie's neck. "We never
would have managed it if you hadn't
been so determined."

They went back to the Treasure Tree and picked delicious fruit and nuts. As the sun set, the happy animals said goodbye and headed for home.

Maisie smiled at all the other animals, but the girls could tell she was worried. "I'm glad that the forest is safe again," she told them, "but I'm still so worried about my mum and Auntie Dappletrot."

"We'll get them back tomorrow, Maisie," said Jess. "Since no time passes in our world while we're in Friendship Forest why don't Goldie, Lily and I stay for a sleepover, so you won't be alone."

The foal's face lit up. "Yes, please!"

"And tomorrow," said Lily, "we're going to save your family!"

Story Two
Thunder Roars

CHAPTER ONE

Mr Cleverfeather's Horseshoes

Jess and Lily woke up to find sunshine streaming through the stable doorway of the Dappletrots' cottage. They'd spent a comfortable night on beds of hay, covered with soft blankets. A delicious smell wafted from the kitchen.

 75

Beside them, Maisie Dappletrot stirred and snuffled. "Mmm, Mum's making apple pancakes for breakfast!" she murmured, and opened her eyes. She looked around the cottage and her face fell as she remembered. "Oh, no! Grizelda took Mum and Auntie away."

Lily cuddled the foal. "We'll find your family today," she said. "We promise."

Goldie came in with a big tray of warm apple pancakes and a jug of milk. "At least the Speedy Weeds have gone," she said. "Now we can concentrate on finding them."

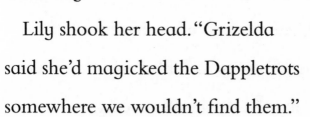

"We don't stop until we do!" Maisie said determinedly.

"They can't be invisible like Captain Ace's balloon, can they?" Goldie said anxiously.

Lily shook her head. "Grizelda said she'd magicked the Dappletrots somewhere we wouldn't find them."

"Let's go to where we saw them last, just before they vanished," said Maisie.

"We might find a clue."

Everyone agreed that was the best idea.
They hurriedly ate breakfast, then Maisie
put on her harness and pulled them
in her cart until they arrived at the
clearing where Grizelda had made the
Dappletrots vanish.

Jess jumped out of the cart and looked
around. "What should we search for?"

But before anyone could answer, the
ground began to tremble under their feet.

"Could that be hoofbeats?" Lily
exclaimed. "Maybe the Dappletrots are
coming back!"

Maisie's mane flew as she shook her head. "Mum or Auntie's hooves would never shake the ground like this …"

With a snort, Thunder the black unicorn charged into the clearing. He reared up on his hind legs, tossing his white horn in the air.

"You'll never find those ponies while I'm around," he said in a booming voice.

The friends cowered as Thunder reared up. He hammered the ground with both his front hooves, making it shake so much that Goldie stumbled, and Lily had to grab a tree trunk to keep herself upright.

Thunder's deep laugh echoed around them – just like thunder in the sky. He slammed his hooves down again and Maisie gave a neigh of fright as her hooves slipped on the shuddering ground.

"We can't search like this," shouted Jess. "Let's go!"

They staggered out of the clearing.

"My legs feel as wobbly as jelly!" cried Maisie. Her little cart was juddering

behind her as she staggered along.

When they were far enough from Thunder's stamping for the tremors to fade, they stopped to get their breath back. Through the bushes, Lily saw a large tree she recognised. It had a ladder winding around the trunk, up to a shed perched in its branches.

"Look!" said Lily. "There's Mr Cleverfeather's inventing shed. Maybe he'll have an invention that can help us."

They hurried to the tree. Mr Cleverfeather the elderly owl was down on the forest floor. He took his monocle

from his
pocket and
peered at the girls.
"Hello! Nice of you to
bop dry," he said, mixing up
his words like he always did.
"I mean, drop by! Did you
all feel the ground shake a
moment ago?"

Jess explained what had
happened. "Thunder is
making it impossible for us
to look for clues," she
told him.

"Do you have something that can help?"

Mr Cleverfeather scratched his chin with one of his wings. "Some Flip-Flop Floaters would be thust the jing," he said. "Just the thing, I mean. They make you float above the ground."

Lily's eyes widened in hope.

"But I haven't invented those yet."

The girls and Goldie shared a disappointed look.

But then Mr Cleverfeather gave a hoot of excitement. "I've got it!" He flew up to his shed, muttering, "I knew they'd come in dandy one hay."

"I think he means 'handy one day',"
said Goldie with a smile.

Moments later Mr Cleverfeather
fluttered back down, holding four silver
horseshoes.

"They're very pretty," said Jess
doubtfully, "but I can't see how they'll
help us find the Dappletrots."

Mr Cleverfeather just smiled and placed
the horseshoes on the ground. "Put your
hooves on those, Maisie."

Maisie placed a hoof on each of the
silver horseshoes. As she did so, two
ribbons curled out from each of them and

tied themselves in a pretty bow, holding the horseshoes to Maisie's feet.

"There!" said Mr Cleverfeather. "Perfect!"

"But Mr Cleverfeather," said Jess, "what do they do?"

Mr Cleverfeather grinned. "Why don't you three all sit in Maisie's cart? Then you'll see!"

The girls and Goldie climbed into the back of the cart.

"Now run, Maisie!" cried Mr Cleverfeather, waving a wing. Maisie cantered forwards as fast as she could.

Then, suddenly, she was galloping

upwards, the cart floating behind her as

she soared into the air.

Jess gasped with amazement. "We're

flying!"

CHAPTER TWO

At Craggy Cliff

Mr Cleverfeather looked like a dot on the ground as they soared over Friendship Forest. Maisie tossed her head joyfully as her long brown mane and tail rippled in the wind.

"I can go really fast when I'm flying!" she cried, happily.

Lily pointed to a huge round tree, towering over the others. "Look! We're higher than the Treasure Tree!"

"It's amazing!" said Goldie. "Now we can search the forest even if Thunder is making the ground shake."

They skimmed over the trees, peering down for any sign of the Dappletrots.

"I can't see Mum and Auntie anywhere," said Maisie with a sigh.

A dark shape at the edge of the forest caught Lily's eye. It was a tall tower with a pointed top, surrounded by ugly grey bushes. She pointed at it.

"There's Grizelda's tower," Lily said. "Maybe she's hidden the Dappletrots somewhere there."

Maisie turned the cart around and headed for the tower. They flew over the rest of the forest, then over the simmering water of the Wide Lake, and soon they were at the tower itself.

Maisie flew in a loop all around it. But the tower was quiet, and everything was completely still.

"I don't think Grizelda's home," whispered Jess, "but I don't think the Dappletrots are here, either."

Goldie pointed to a jagged, rocky cliff soaring up behind the tower. A rickety old bridge led from a clump of spiky trees at the very top, across the Wide Lake and back to Friendship Forest. "That's Craggy Cliff," she said. "And look what's at the top of it."

Close to the spiky trees was a gloomy brown building.

"The Dappletrots could be in there," said Jess. "Let's look."

Maisie turned the cart towards Craggy Cliff. The bridge that connected it to the forest was creaking as it swayed in the wind. Lily shuddered as they flew over it.

"I'm glad we don't have to walk across that," she said. "It looks like it could fall down at any minute!"

Maisie landed her cart behind the spiky trees. The girls and Goldie climbed out, and they crept carefully towards the building. It was like a big wooden shed with high windows.

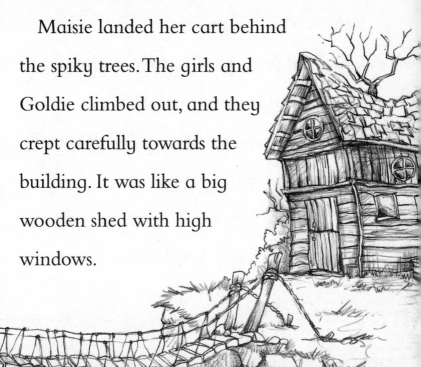

"It's a stable!" cried Lily. "That has to be where the Dappletrots are!"

"The unicorns might be there, too," whispered Goldie, her ears twitching nervously. "We'd better be quiet."

The little group crept towards the stable. Jess tried the door handle. It was locked.

She jumped up to try to look through a window, but it was too high.

"How can we see if anyone's in there?" Goldie wondered.

"Let's climb on this," said Lily softly. She dragged a big wooden box over to

the window. Stuck to the side was a label that said "Bitter Berries".

"Bitter Berries – yuck!" whispered Maisie. "No wonder those unicorns are cross, if that's what Grizelda feeds them."

The four friends stood on the box and peeked through the grimy window. Inside, the stable was dark and gloomy.

There was a pile of damp-looking hay,
a bucket of water … and two ponies!

"Mum!" Maisie shouted, too delighted
to be quiet. "Auntie!"

Mrs Dappletrot trotted to the window,
whinnying happily. "Maisie, darling! I've
been so worried. Are you all right?"

"Yes," said the foal. "Lily, Jess and
Goldie are looking after me. I'm so happy
we've found you!"

"We'll get you out," said Lily.

"Grizelda locked us in here with a
huge rusty key," said Auntie Dappletrot.
"I think you'll need to find it."

"We'll loo—" Jess began, then she froze.

So did the others, as they heard the sound of galloping hooves.

Lily jumped down and peered around the side of the stable. Her heart raced as she saw that Thunder, Lightning and Stormcloud were cantering towards them.

"It's the unicorns!" she cried. "Quick! Everyone hide!"

CHAPTER THREE

Inside Grizelda's Tower

"Go!" cried Mrs Dappletrot. "Quickly! We'll be all right."

Jess and Goldie jumped off the Bitter Berries box and stood next to Lily.

"Maisie! Come on!" Lily said urgently.

The foal galloped after the others. But she was too slow! Lightning spotted her and gave a snort of fury.

"Hey, you!" he yelled. "Get back here!"

The four friends sprinted to the spiky trees. Maisie scrambled into her harness once more, and the girls and Goldie jumped into the cart just as Lightning and Stormcloud charged around the trees, their horns lowered.

"Fly, Maisie!" cried Goldie. "Hurry!"

Maisie galloped over the ground for a few paces, then her hooves were stepping onto air and they flew up. The three unicorns stared after the little cart as they soared away.

Goldie and the girls held tight as the cart swooped from side to side.

"We need that key," Maisie called over her shoulder. Her voice was shaking, but she gave a determined toss of her mane. "So we're going to Grizelda's tower and we're going to find it!"

She landed the cart behind some tall, spiky thistles and ducked out of her harness.

Close by came the *click* of high-heeled-shoe footsteps.

"Grizelda!" whispered Jess. "She must just be arriving home."

They ducked behind the thistles. Grizelda came into view, her cloak swishing behind her. She seemed even grumpier than usual.

"My lovely Speedy Weeds are gone," she muttered to herself, as she made her way to the tower door. "I know what will cheer me up – I'll write some new spells."

As she went inside, the side of her cloak

flicked around to show a pocket – with
a big rusty key sticking out of it. She
slammed the door shut behind her.

"That must be the key we need!"
whispered Lily.

They crept across the
grey, muddy ground
to the tower door.
Carefully, trying to
be as quiet as she
could, Jess turned
the handle and they
crept inside. It smelled
of stale air and mould.

Maisie flew, so her hooves wouldn't clatter on the stone floor.

They tiptoed up the cobwebby spiral staircase to a hallway with doors on each side. The friends stopped at each one, listening for Grizelda.

Finally, Lily heard something. She beckoned the others over and they peeped through a crack.

Grizelda was sitting at a desk, writing in a book. Nearby, a cauldron bubbled and puffed out dirty green smoke. Her cloak was slung over a high-backed chair – and the key sticking out of the pocket!

"How can we get it?" whispered Jess.

"I know!" Maisie whispered. "I bet if Grizelda thought Mum and Auntie had got free, she'd rush outside so quickly that she might forget her cloak! Maybe if I make enough noise to sound like two ponies, I can fool her!"

"Brilliant!" whispered Lily. "But be careful, Maisie."

Maisie nodded and flew silently down the stairs while the girls and Goldie hid in a shadowy corner.

After a few moments, they heard Maisie's hoofbeats and neighs coming from outside.

Grizelda's door flew open and the witch stomped out. "Those ponies have escaped!" she shrieked.

Lily and Jess both held their breath. Would the plan work?

CHAPTER FOUR

Pony Rescue!

"Don't think you can get away from me, silly ponies!" Grizelda shouted, as she ran down the stairs.

"Maisie's done it!" Lily whispered with delight. "Grizelda's forgotten her cloak!"

Jess ran into the room and grabbed the key out of the pocket in Grizelda's cloak.

 105

She waved it in the air.

"We've got it!"

"Hurry!" said Goldie, starting downstairs. "We must make sure Grizelda doesn't catch Maisie!"

As they ran out of the tower, they saw Grizelda charging into the forest.

"I know you're there, you wretched ponies!" she shrieked. Then she shouted even louder. "Unicorns! Where are you?

Why aren't you here when I need you?"

"I hope Maisie's not in those trees," said Goldie. "She might not be fast enough to get away. Where is she?"

A soft whinny came from far above them.

They looked up to see Maisie perched right at the top of Grizelda's tower! She flew down to join them.

"I knew Grizelda wouldn't think to look up in the air," Maisie explained.

"Very clever!" said Jess, ruffling her mane. "Now, let's go and save your family!"

Moments later, they were flying back to Craggy Cliff. There was no sign of the unicorns.

"They must have gone to see what Grizelda wanted," said Goldie.

Maisie landed next to the stable and the friends ran to the stable door. Jess turned the key in the lock.

Clunk!

The door opened. Mrs Dappletrot and Auntie rushed out and the three ponies nuzzled one another, their tails swishing as they neighed with joy. The girls and Goldie grinned.

"We'd better go," said Goldie, "before Grizelda realises she's been tricked."

Maisie was showing her mum her magic horseshoes. But then her face fell. "But I'm too little to carry everyone in my cart. What are we going to do?"

Jess looked over at the cliff edge, to where the rickety bridge was creaking and swaying. It was made of short planks of wood roped together, and two other ropes made handrails. Many of the planks were split and broken. Jess glanced at Lily, and knew that they were thinking the same thing.

"Goldie, Mrs Dappletrot and Auntie can go in your cart," Jess said with a gulp. "Lily and I will go over the bridge."

"But it looks so dangerous," said Goldie. "Why don't we take it in turns for Maisie to carry us over in the cart?"

But then they heard the thunder of hooves behind them.

"There's no time," said Lily, grabbing onto the side of the bridge. "Let's go!"

CHAPTER FIVE

The Rickety Bridge

Jess and Lily made their way along the bridge, holding hands and going as quickly as they dared. The planks were covered in sharp splinters and they had to watch their step to avoid the broken ones. Far below the bridge, the water of the Wide Lake glittered.

 111

"Don't look down, Lily," said Jess.

Maisie flew beside them, her mum, Auntie and Goldie squashed into the cart.

Goldie's eyes were wide with worry.

"You're nearly there!" she called out to them. The bridge creaked and groaned, but the girls kept going. The forest was close now. The sun was starting to set, making the tops of the trees

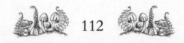

glow golden, and Jess could see wisps of chimney smoke coming from some of the cottages.

But then the bridge shook from side to side. Lily and Jess both screamed and clung to the handrails. When Lily looked around, she could see Thunder coming over the bridge towards them!

"Help!" cried Jess.

Thunder stamped on the planks. The bridge rocked horribly again.

She and Jess clung desperately to the ropes holding up the bridge.

"We'll fall!" cried Lily.

Then, to the girls' surprise, Maisie gave a furious neigh.

"Go away, you mean unicorn!" she yelled. "I won't let you hurt my family, and I won't let you hurt my friends, either!"

Then she dipped her little head and galloped through the air, heading straight at Thunder.

Goldie and the Dappletrots held on to the cart as Maisie galloped through the air as fast as she could.

"Go away!" she yelled again.

Thunder give a whinny of shock. He turned around and started cantering away from the cross little pony, back over the bridge towards Craggy Cliff.

Lily and Jess cheered as Maisie turned the cart around. The girls hurried over the rest of the bridge, then jumped off safely onto solid ground. Maisie landed her cart beside them and the girls threw their arms around her.

"You saved us!" cried Lily.

"Nothing stops Maisie," said Jess, with a laugh. "Not even a horrible unicorn!"

They made their way back through the forest to the Dappletrots' stable. Though the Speedy Weeds had gone, the buds that covered the trees and bushes were still closed.

"We'll need to find more Grow Gems so they can open," said Auntie Dappletrot.

"I think we could all do with some dinner first," said Mrs Dappletrot. "I'll make us all some carrot stew."

"My favourite!" said Maisie.

 117

Stars were starting to appear as the sun set. The trees cast soft shadows around them. "Let's collect the Grow Gems in the morning," said Goldie.

Jess nodded, fighting back a yawn. "We'll need a good rest," she said. "We've saved the forest and the Dappletrots – and tomorrow we've got to save Beautiful Bloom Day!"

Story Three
Stormcloud
Rushes In

CHAPTER ONE

The Dappletrots' Secret

"Where am I?" Jess mumbled to herself when she woke up the next morning. With a thrill of excitement, she remembered that she had slept over in Freindship Forest again, in the Dappletrots' cottage, with Lily and Goldie. Today they had to find Grow Gems to

sprinkle under all the trees and bushes,
so the flowers would open and spring
would begin!

Lily opened her eyes. "I'd never have
thought a hay bed could be so snuggly
and warm," she murmured sleepily,
cuddling down beneath her blanket.

Maisie trotted around the door.

 122

"You're awake!" she said. "Mum's made breakfast!"

Soon, the girls, Goldie and all the Dappletrots were enjoying creamy porridge oats, topped with honey and blueberries.

"Imagine being one of Grizelda's unicorns, and having to eat Bitter Berries for breakfast," said Maisie.

Mrs Dappletrot looked worried. "I hope the unicorns stay away while we collect more Grow Gems."

"Is it easy to get Grow Gems?" Lily asked her.

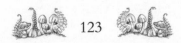

Mrs Dappletrot glanced at Auntie, who nodded and said, "Goldie and the girls deserve to know the secret. So does Maisie. They've all been so brave."

Everyone looked at Mrs Dappletrot.

"The location of the gems is hidden from the rest of the forest," she said, "because they're so important."

"They grow in a secret garden," Auntie continued. "Only Dappletrots with green jewel necklaces know where it is. Only when a pony is fully grown-up are they given their necklace, and told where the secret garden is."

Maisie looked down longingly at the ring of flowers around her neck.

Lily patted her side comfortingly. "Your flowers are lovely, too," she whispered.

"But today," Mrs Dappletrot said, "we'll all go to the garden, because we must collect the gems before the unicorns can stop us."

Little Maisie squealed with excitement and kicked up her heels.

After breakfast, the ponies hitched up
their carts. Goldie and Lily rode with Mrs
Dappletrot, and Jess with Auntie. Maisie
put her magical horseshoes in her cart
and followed behind.

As they hurried through the forest,
Lily looked at branches heavy with buds,
nodding in the breeze. "It'll be terrible if
they never open," she said to Goldie. "If
there are no flowers, there'll be no food
on the Treasure Tree either, and everyone
will have to leave the forest!"

"We'll make sure they bloom," Goldie
said determinedly.

After a while, Jess
realised that Auntie
Dappletrot was heading
straight for a thick curtain of
ivy. It was so dark, she was
certain that there must be
a wall behind it. She was
about to shout, "Watch
out!" when Auntie
Dappletrot put her
head down and
walked right
through
it.

A long grassy path lay before them, shaded by weeping willow trees.

Goldie stared. "I've never been to this part of the forest before!" she said.

At the end of the path was a huge garden filled with flowerbeds. While the ponies unhitched their carts, Lily took a closer look. They were filled with little plants that had fluffy heads, just like dandelion clocks.

"I can't see any Grow Gems," she said to Jess. "I wonder where they are?"

The ponies had taken a heap of gardening tools from a nearby shed. There was a spade, some little garden forks and a plough.

"Auntie's going to show you all how to find Grow Gems," said Mrs Dappletrot. "Take a little garden fork each."

They all did. Maisie was swishing her tail around in excitement, clutching the fork in her mouth.

Auntie Dappletrot stood in front of one of the plants.

"These are Gemflowers," she explained. "They mark the spot where a Grow Gem can be found."

Lily grinned. "So we've just got to dig

them up?" She waved an arm over the
carpet of Gemflowers. "We'll have loads
of them in no time."

Auntie shook her head. "I'm afraid it's
not that easy." She nudged the Gemflower
with her nose. "Come and look."

Maisie, Goldie and the girls peered
down at it. The flower's centre flashed and
glittered in the sunshine, like a diamond.

"Wow!" said Jess. "That's beautiful!"

"That sparkle means there's a gem
underneath," said Auntie. "If there's no
sparkle, a gem hasn't grown yet. We can't
just pull them all up, otherwise there

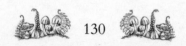

won't be any
Grow Gems for
next year. Check
each flower
before you dig."

"Let's get
going!" said Mrs
Dappletrot.

They stepped in among the
Gemflowers. Lily crouched down to look
at a flower. The centre dazzled red like
a ruby.

"Got one!" she cried. As she dug, it
started to rain – heavier and heavier.

"This is no ordinary rain," Goldie said grimly.

Lily and Jess looked up. Sure enough, the blue sky was now covered with blankets of dark grey clouds. The rain was getting worse with each passing second.

"Keep going!" Mrs Dappletrot yelled.

But before the others could reply, a grey unicorn galloped through the curtain of ivy and into the secret garden.

"Oh, no!" cried Jess. "It's Stormcloud!"

CHAPTER TWO

Stuck in the Mud!

Jess grabbed Lily's hand. They were both already drenched from the rain, their hair sticking to their faces. The ponies' coats were sopping wet and their tails drooped.

Stormcloud laughed and flicked his tail menacingly. As he did so, the grey clouds grew darker and the rain fell even harder.

 133

It battered the Gemflowers so much that they were flattened against the ground.

"Oh, no!" cried Lily. "We won't be able to tell where the gems are!"

Stormcloud whinnied with delight. "It was so clever of me to follow you here!" he boasted. "Now it'll never be spring in the forest!"

He flicked his tail again and the rain stopped as suddenly as it had started. Then, with a wicked neigh, he cantered away.

The friends stared at the flowerbeds in dismay. They had turned into gloopy pools of mud with broken Gemflowers floating in them.

Mrs Dappletrot had tears in her eyes. "However will we find the gems now?"

Maisie gave a determined stamp of her hooves. "We've got to try!" The little pony jumped back onto the path and galloped towards the pile of gardening equipment. "I know," she cried. "We could use the plough!"

"But what about the rest of the Grow Gem flowers?" Jess asked.

"They're all ruined anyway," Lily said sadly.

"We'll just have to work extra hard to grow more in time for next year," Mrs Dappletrot said, "but, right now, we have to get those Grow Gems!" She trotted over to the plough and got into the harness.

But when she tried to pull it through the flowerbed, her hooves slipped and skidded in the mud.

"It's no good," she cried eventually. "If only I could fit into your flying horseshoes," she sighed.

"I can pull the plough!" Maisie cried.

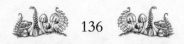

"It's a lovely idea, Maisie," said her mum, "but the plough's just too heavy for you."

The foal tossed her mane. "I can do it," she said. "I've got to, so we can save Friendship Forest."

Jess grinned. "If anyone can," she said, "it's Maisie."

Lily nodded. "She's the most determined little pony ever!"

Maisie hitched herself to the plough. Then she put on the magical horseshoes.

She flew over the flowerbed, staying so low that the plough dragged through

the mud. The plough churned up the mud, throwing soggy Gemflowers to the surface.

"Look!" cried Lily. She darted towards the path left by the plough to grab something shiny. It was a brilliant blue Grow Gem!

"Keep going, Maisie!" cried Goldie.

As the plough turned the mud over, more sparkling gems of every colour appeared.

The girls and Goldie ran along behind, stepping as lightly as they could on the mud as they picked up handfuls of gems and piled them into the carts. Mrs and Auntie Dappletrot tapped their hooves to the magical beat and Grow Gems flew through the air.

"You've done a wonderful job," Mrs Dappletrot said, looking at the carts full of Grow Gems.

"Now let's go and sprinkle them around the forest quickly, before Stormcloud comes back," Auntie Dappletrot added.

Maisie slipped out from the plough's harness and went over to pull the little cart. Off they set down the path that led from the garden back to the forest. But then Mrs Dappletrot jerked to a halt. She sank into the mud, up to her knees.

"Oh, no!" cried Mrs Dappletrot, wriggling around. "I'm stuck!"

"Me, too!" said Auntie, tossing her head. Jess stared at the ground with a groan.

"Stormcloud must have made it rain here, too," Lily said gloomily.

Auntie and Mrs Dappletrot leaned forwards, pulling desperately, with Goldie

and the girls pushing. The two carts
moved for a few more steps, but then they
were stuck again.

"Don't worry," Jess said to the two
ponies. "We'll get you out."

They pulled, then pushed as hard as
they could, but they could only move the
ponies a tiny bit.

"What are we going to do?" asked Mrs Dappletrot. "We're stuck fast. Maisie, you can fly above the path – you're going to have to scatter the Grow Gems."

"But how will I be able to do the magic without you?" Maisie asked Mrs Dappletrot.

Maisie's mum looked at Maisie lovingly and said, "You've seen us do it so many times now, I'll bet you can do it all by yourself. I believe in you, Maisie!"

"Us, too!" said the girls.

"OK, I'll try!" Maisie said.

The gems were soon shifted from the

 142

bigger carts to Maisie's smaller one, and the girls filled their pockets, too.

"Auntie and I will catch up as soon as we can," said Mrs Dappletrot, as she struggled in the mud. "Hurry, Maisie!"

The little pony took off and Goldie and the girls ran behind, shouting encouragement.

Goldie darted ahead and held back the ivy curtain so Maisie could fly through, back into the forest.

Maisie landed in front of a bush that was heavy with buds that were ready to bloom. She took a deep breath, then

tapped out the special rhythm with her hooves, just like her mum did. A handful of gems shot out from her cart and scattered under the nearest trees. The magic was working!

"Come on, everyone!" called Maisie. "Let's sprinkle these Grow Gems!"

CHAPTER THREE

Unicorn Storm

Maisie flew between the trees, tapping
her hooves in the air, while the girls and
Goldie grabbed gems from the cart
and raced around sprinkling them. Lily
placed a glittering pink gem underneath
a bush, and its buds immediately bloomed
open to reveal gorgeous, soft pink roses.

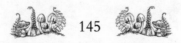

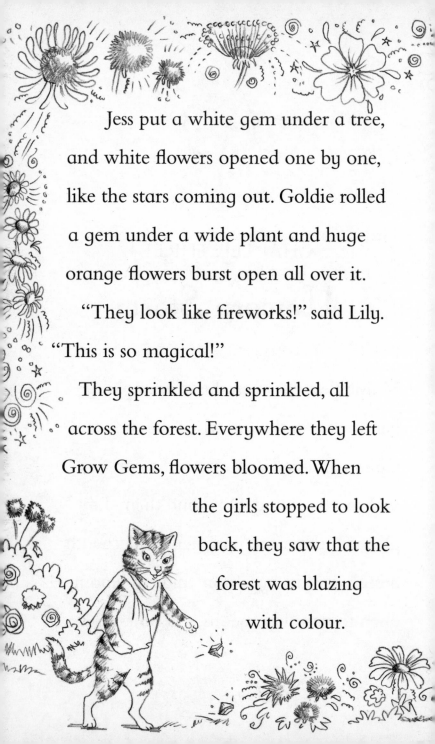

Jess put a white gem under a tree, and white flowers opened one by one, like the stars coming out. Goldie rolled a gem under a wide plant and huge orange flowers burst open all over it.

"They look like fireworks!" said Lily. "This is so magical!"

They sprinkled and sprinkled, all across the forest. Everywhere they left Grow Gems, flowers bloomed. When the girls stopped to look back, they saw that the forest was blazing with colour.

"It's working!" cried Maisie. She danced her hooves in the air with excitement.

Jess was reaching into the cart for more Grow Gems when a fierce wind blew up from behind her, and the thunderous sound of hoofbeats filled the air. "Look out, everyone!" she cried.

Grizelda came crashing through the trees in her chariot, pulled by the three unicorns. "Urgh!" she screeched.

Her green hair whipped around her and she shook her fist angrily. "There are horrible flowers everywhere! Give me those Grow Gems now!"

"Run!" cried Lily.

The four friends raced deep into the forest. Behind them Grizelda shrieked, "Unicorns, stop them! Work together to make a thunderstorm — a really bad one!"

The neighs of the unicorns echoed through the trees. Then the sky darkened and rain fell in heavy drops.

Boooooom! A roll of thunder rumbled.

Cra-a-ck! A streak of lightning flashed.

Maisie jumped with fright. Her cart nearly toppled over, but the girls grabbed it and kept it upright.

"It's all right!" Jess yelled over the noise of the storm. "Let's keep going!"

The girls were soaked, Goldie's fur was drenched, and Maisie's mane was stuck to her face, but there was one Grow Gem left, the biggest one of them all.

"That's for the Treasure Tree!" Maisie gasped. "Come on!"

The girls and Goldie climbed into the almost-empty cart and Maisie galloped on, pulling the cart through the air.

Through the rain they could see the top of the Treasure Tree, with lightning flashing round it. Maisie picked up speed, then stopped her cart at the foot of its trunk. Fat drops of rainwater were dripping from the buds that hung on the branches.

Lily picked up the last Grow Gem – a sparkling diamond – and leaped from the cart. She hurled it among the Treasure Tree's roots.

The branches quivered and then, in spite of the dark and the rain, the tree burst into blossom. The girls gasped as flowers of every colour covered the tree so that it looked as bright as a rainbow.

"Hooray!" Maisie cried. "We've beaten Grizelda!"

CHAPTER FOUR

A Sparkling Jewel

The friends hugged one another.

"Not even Grizelda's unicorns could stop you, Maisie!" said Goldie.

"That's because they're useless!" shouted a furious voice. Grizelda rode up beside the Treasure Tree, still pulled in her chariot by the three unicorns. "Agh! Stop this storm! My hair's all wet!"

The three unicorns tossed their horns.
The rain slowed to a trickle, the thunder
stopped and the black clouds and
lightning disappeared.

Grizelda leaped down. Her green hair
dripped over her tunic and rain ran down
her face.

"You failed me!" Grizelda shrieked at
the unicorns. "I should have given you
more Bitter Berries. Then you might have
stopped those interfering girls!"

While Grizelda carried on shouting
and screaming, Lily suddenly had an idea.

She whispered to Jess and Goldie, "Maybe the unicorns are only horrible because Grizelda feeds them Bitter Berries."

Jess nodded. "Yes! Remember the Quite Contrary potion?"

"We could do the same thing for the unicorns!" Goldie finished. "We haven't got time to make a potion, but if we give them something that's the opposite of Bitter Berries, it might make them nice."

Grizelda was still yelling at the unicorns and shaking her fists, so they turned to the Treasure Tree.

Goldie found some tiny, juicy grapes

and Jess picked honeyberries. Lily filled
her pockets with custard apples, which
had delicious custard in the middle
instead of pips.

"I hope this works," whispered Lily.
"If it doesn't, we'll be facing three angry
unicorns!"

Goldie and the girls approached the
unicorns quietly. Grizelda had turned to
the Treasure Tree and was kicking it with
her high-heeled boot.

"Are you hungry, Thunder?" Lily asked
nervously. She held out a custard apple
and offered it to him.

Thunder crunched the apple. "Yum!" he said. "More, please!"

Lightning took Jess's honeyberries and Stormcloud munched the little grapes, squirting juice everywhere.

"Much nicer than Grizelda's berries!" he said.

"Delicious!" boomed Thunder.

"Stop eating those!" Grizelda shrieked.

She ran towards them but stopped when silver sparkles appeared, showering over the three unicorns. Their manes and tails gleamed snow-white, and their horns and hooves shone silver.

The three unicorns stared down at themselves in wonder.

"We're ourselves again!" cried Lightning.

"Thank you!" cried Thunder. "My *real* name is Rumble, and this is Raindrop and Flash." He pointed to Stormcloud and Lightning in turn. The two other unicorns nodded their heads at the girls.

Raindrop marched up to Grizelda, who was backing away from them. "You tricked us into stopping by your tower!" he said. "We were on our way to our homes on the Ivory Horn, and you pretended to be our friend."

"Your Bitter Berries turned us bad," said Flash.

"But the spell's broken," said Rumble. "We're not helping you any more!"

They charged at Grizelda and she fled, splashing away through the mud. "Horrid pony!" she shrieked, stumbling through the trees. "Horrid cat! Horrid unicorns!

And you interfering girls are the most horrid of all!"

As she ran out of sight, the unicorns turned to the girls. "We didn't mean to cause such trouble," said Raindrop.

"We understand," said Lily.

"As thanks for helping us get away from Grizelda, we hope you'll accept this gift," said Flash. The three unicorns joined their horns and, a moment later, the sky was filled with the biggest, most beautiful rainbow the girls had ever seen.

"Happy Beautiful Bloom Day, everyone!" said Maisie, with a whinny of delight.

Later that day, everyone gathered at the Dappletrots' home. The cottage was decorated with flowers, and the whole

161

forest was gloriously in bloom. Mrs Dappletrot and Auntie Dappletrot had made their way home and had a bath to get rid of the mud. They had flowers woven into their manes and tail, and Maisie had taken off her flower garland and instead had flowers in her mane, just like her mum.

"What is everyone doing here?" asked Lily in surprise.

"We're having a party," Maisie explained. "To celebrate the beginning of spring."

"How lovely!" cried Jess.

Mr Cleverfeather, Captain Ace, Poppy Muddlepup and lots of the girls' animal friends were there. The three unicorns had stayed, too, each with a flower tucked behind one of their ears.

"But today we're celebrating something else, too," Mrs Dappletrot said. "Maisie, would you come here, please?"

The foal did as she was told, looking nervous. Jess and Lily joined everyone else, waiting to hear what Mrs Dappletrot had to say.

"Maisie Dappletrot," she began. "You're a brave, determined pony. With your friends, you saved Friendship Forest from Grizelda. You've proved you're grown-up enough to be a true Dappletrot!"

Coloured sparkles rose up from the ground and showered down over Maisie.

When they cleared, everyone gasped.

"Look!" cried Lily.

Maisie glanced down. Her mouth

fell open in surprise. A sparkling green

jewel hung around her neck from a silver

necklace!

"Hooray!"

cheered Jess.

Everyone cheered

Maisie. She hopped

from hoof to hoof

and kept looking

down to admire

her jewel.

Then Mrs Dappletrot called, "Unicorns! I know you must be heading back to your home, but won't you visit us again sometime?"

The unicorns nodded, prancing in delight. Their silver horns and hooves flashed brightly in the sunlight.

"We promise not to make trouble again," said Flash. "Oh, I forgot! I'm sorry I made Captain Ace's balloon disappear." He pointed his silver horn into the sky.

Instantly, the balloon reappeared.

"Thank you!" cried the stork.

"And we'll fix the flowers we ruined,"

added Rumble, "so there'll be plenty of Grow Gems for next year."

"And I'll be there to scatter them around the forest," Maisie said proudly.

After lots of singing, dancing, unicorn rides and balloon trips, it was time for the girls to go home.

The Dappletrots hugged them. "Thanks for everything," they said.

"We'll see you again soon," said Lily.

As they left, Maisie gave them each a Grow Gem. "These are for you."

Lily's gem was cherry red and Jess's shone gleaming gold.

"Thanks!" they said in delight.

The girls said their goodbyes and Goldie led them back to the Friendship Tree. She touched her paw to the trunk, and a door appeared.

Jess opened it, letting the familiar golden light spill out.

She hugged Goldie. "Come and get us if Grizelda causes trouble again," she said.

"Of course I will," said Goldie, giving Lily a hug.

"Goodbye. See you soon."

The girls stepped into the golden light, and felt the tingle that meant they were returning to their normal size. When the light faded, they found themselves in Brightley Meadow.

"Wow!" said Lily. "What a brilliant adventure!"

They ran back to Helping Paw. As they reached the little vegetable garden, Jess said, "Hmmmm, I wonder if these Grow Gems would help our garden grow?"

Lily grinned. "Let's plant them and see!"

They pushed them deep into the soil.

169

Instantly, their carrot seedlings grew tall, the green leaves long and feathery.

Lily pulled one up. A bright orange carrot came out of the ground.

"Wow! That's magical!" said Jess. She pulled another one.

"I know just what to do with these," said Lily.

Moments later, two grey Shetland ponies were munching happily on two delicious – and magical – carrots!

The End

Wicked witch Grizelda is causing trouble at Shimmer Lake! Can Jess, Lily and little kitten Katie Prettywhiskers stop her and her horrid new helpers?

Turn over for a sneak peek of the next adventure,

Katie Prettywhiskers To the Rescue

"Why are you doing this?" Jess asked. "The Sapphire Isle's no use to you!"

Grizelda scowled. "It is!" she shrieked. "I'll name it Sorcery Isle, and I'll build a holiday tower by the beach."

"We'll stop you!" Lily told her.

"You won't," Grizelda sneered. "My new servants will make sure of it."

Four tiny creatures sprang out from behind Grizelda and landed on the jetty.

"Meet my water imps," said Grizelda.

The imps stood as tall as the girls' ankles. They had blue skin and wore hats, tattered trousers and stripy tops. One of them carried a net made from seaweed.

"Ahoy there, land lubbers!" he cried.

"That's Kelp," said Grizelda.

"They're like little pirates," Lily whispered to Jess. "Kelp's even got a wooden leg!"

The second imp patted her tummy.

"Ain't it lunchtime yet?" she asked. "I could eat a whole pondweed cake!"

Read

Katie Prettywhiskers To the Rescue

to find out what happens next!

Magic
Animal Friends

Look out for the brand-new
Magic Animal Friends series!

Series Five

www.magicanimalfriends.com

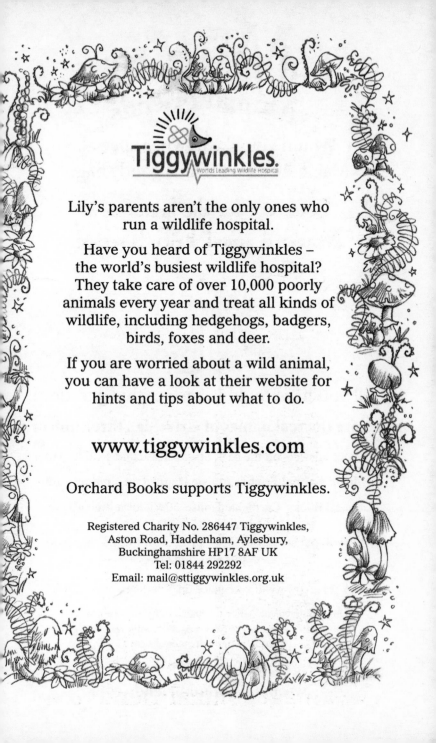

Tiggywinkles.
Worlds Leading Wildlife Hospital

Lily's parents aren't the only ones who run a wildlife hospital.

Have you heard of Tiggywinkles – the world's busiest wildlife hospital? They take care of over 10,000 poorly animals every year and treat all kinds of wildlife, including hedgehogs, badgers, birds, foxes and deer.

If you are worried about a wild animal, you can have a look at their website for hints and tips about what to do.

www.tiggywinkles.com

Orchard Books supports Tiggywinkles.

Registered Charity No. 286447 Tiggywinkles,
Aston Road, Haddenham, Aylesbury,
Buckinghamshire HP17 8AF UK
Tel: 01844 292292
Email: mail@sttiggywinkles.org.uk

Magic
Animal Friends

Would you like to win a special
Magic Animal Friends goody bag?

All you have to do is answer this question:

What are the real names of Grizelda's three unicorns?

Put your answers on the back of a postcard and send it to us at

Magic Animal Friends Maisie Dappletrot Competition

Orchard Books, Carmelite House, 50 Victoria Embankment
London, EC4Y 0DZ
We will put all entries into a prize draw for the chance to
win this amazing prize!

A prize draw will take place on 30th September 2016

Competition open to UK and Republic of Ireland residents only.
No purchase necessary. For full terms and conditions please go to
www.hachettechildrens.co.uk/terms

Good Luck!

www.magicanimalfriends.com